Stornoway Primary School
Jamieson Drive
Stornoway
Isle of Lewis
HS1 2LF
Tel: 01851 703418/703621
Fax: 01851 706257
E Mail: stornoway-primary@cne-siar.gov.uk

CAPTAIN ABDUL'S PIRATE SCHOOL

Colin McNaughton has written and illustrated many books for children, including *Have You Seen Who's Just Moved In Next Door To Us?* (Winner of the Kurt Maschler Award) and *Here Come the Aliens!* (shortlisted for the Kate Greenaway Medal), *Jolly Roger*, *Dracula's Tomb* and a collection of tales about Preston Pig. His four hugely popular poetry titles, including the hilarious collection about disastrous holidays, *Wish You Were Here (And I Wasn't)*, are all now available on audio cassette, read by Colin himself.

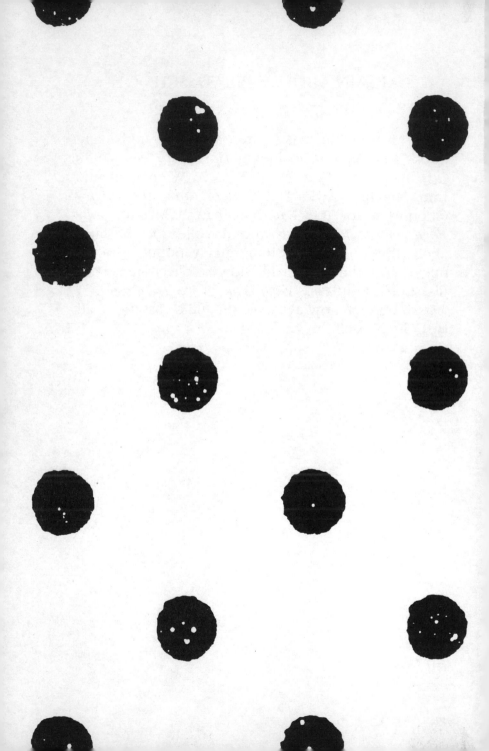

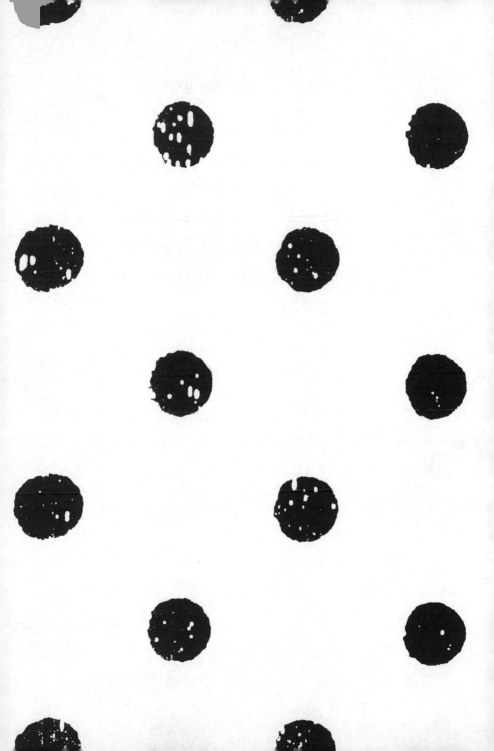

Books by the same author

Jolly Roger

*There's an Awful Lot of Weirdos
in Our Neighbourhood*

Making Friends with Frankenstein

Who's Been Sleeping in My Porridge?

Wish You Were Here (And I Wasn't)

CAPTAIN ABDUL'S PIRATE SCHOOL

For Rocky Lawson,
the first pirate I ever met

First published 1994 by Walker Books Ltd
87 Vauxhall Walk, London SE11 5HJ

Sprinters edition published 2001

Sprinters edition published in hardback by Heinemann Library,
a division of Reed Educational and Professional Publishing Limited,
by arrangement with Walker Books Ltd

© 1994, 2001 Colin McNaughton

This book has been typeset in Garamond 3

Printed in Great Britain by
St Edmundsbury Press, Bury St Edmunds

British Library Cataloguing in Publication Data:
a catalogue record for this book
is available from the British Library

0-431-01791-3

CAPTAIN ABDUL'S PIRATE SCHOOL

COLIN MᶜNAUGHTON

WALKER BOOKS
AND SUBSIDIARIES
LONDON • BOSTON • SYDNEY

Dear Diary,

Well, here I stinking am! My first stinking day at Captain Abdul's Pirate School. My stinking dad has sent me here because he says I'm a big softie! (Just because I like writing poems and painting pictures!) He says it will toughen me up. He says a kid my age should jump at the chance of becoming a pirate. He says that when he was a kid he wanted to be a pirate and so should I.

He says I should be grateful.

Well, I say, "Nuts!" and I say, "Steaming cowdung!" and I say, "I hope he swallows his pipe!"

P.S. I have a secret.

I have smuggled my little dog Spud in my trunk. He's the only friend I've got in the whole stinking world!

We were met at the door by
Captain Abdul himself: hairy,
scary and with more bits missing
than a second-hand jigsaw.

"Follow me upstairs, me little buccaneers," said Captain Abdul, "an' we'll get yer kit stowed away, ooh-arrgh, that we will. Ha-har, ooh-arrgh!"

Hammocks ~ ooh-arrgh!

Later, Captain Abdul took us

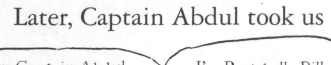

I'm Captain Abdul,
that I be.
An' I'm in charge –
The boss – that's me.
I make the tea and sandwiches
An' teaches foreign
languages!

I'm Portobello Billy,
me.
I teaches pirate
history!

I'm I'm Alright Jack,
That I be.
A teacher of maths
an' geography!

4

to meet the other teachers...

Next we were given our school
uniforms and told to introduce
ourselves.

Jim
Silver

Françoise
du Plonk

Ching
Yih

Ali
Khoja

Unfortunately, Spud thought this included him! Luckily the captain likes dogs and said he could stay (for a small fee).

Henry
Morgan

Rosemary
Lavender

Pickles

Woof!

Spud

I was a bit nervous about meeting the other kids but they don't seem too bad – they look just as miserable as me.

Tom Tew

Anne Bonney

Frankie Drake

Samuel P. Chop

We then had supper and went to bed, where I wrote this and cried a bit for my mum.

Jack Rackam

Simon Smee

Ben Gunn

Bartholomew
Sharp

Mary Read

Beryl Flynn

Dear Diary,

Woke up this morning and stood up in bed. Forgot I was in a hammock – bit of a headache. I was brushing my teeth when Bully-boy McCoy came in.

"What yer doin' that for?" he asked.

"If I don't, sir, my teeth will go black and fall out," I replied.

"What's wrong with that?" he said. "Who ever heard of a pirate with nice teeth!" And he confiscated my toothbrush!

Today we studied history.
Portobello Billy told us an exciting
story about Calico Jack the pirate,
set in his favourite place –
the West Indies.

Dear Diary,

We were queueing for breakfast this morning when Walker the Plank came over and asked Rosemary Lavender if she was pushing in.

"Yes, sir," admitted Rosemary.

"Well done!" said Walker the Plank and walked away.

Today's lessons were maths and geography. In maths we learned about angles. (You use them when aiming cannon.) In geography we learned where the West Indies are and how to read treasure maps.

Dear Diary,

The beastly Captain Abdul has scolded me for being too neat and tidy. He suspects me of brushing my hair –

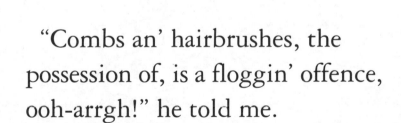

"Combs an' hairbrushes, the possession of, is a floggin' offence, ooh-arrgh!" he told me.

Today we had arts and crafts. We learned how to make cannon balls, swords, fake money and how to put model ships into rum bottles. (Spanish Omar Lette very kindly emptied the bottles for us.)

Dear Diary,

Last night we were doing our homework when Riff-raff Rafferty came in and caught little Simon Smee copying from another boy.

"Was you cheatin', boy?" howled Riff-raff.

"Yes, sir," said Simon Smee in a small voice.

"Good boy!" yelled the teacher. "Go to the top of the class!"

35

36

Today we learned how to speak
pirate. Can't wait till next week's
lesson. It's pirate swearwords!
Ooh-arrgh!

Dear Diary,

The teachers had a party last night! They kept coming up and saying it was much too early to be in bed and why weren't we having a midnight feast or rampaging round the town looking for trouble!

"Why, when I was your age," said the captain, "I already had a wooden leg! Ooh-arrgh!"

When he finally woke up today he bellowed, "Fresh air is what we need, ooh-arrgh! We're goin' to sea!" For the rest of the day we sailed around the harbour in the *Golden Behind*, learning pirate stuff.

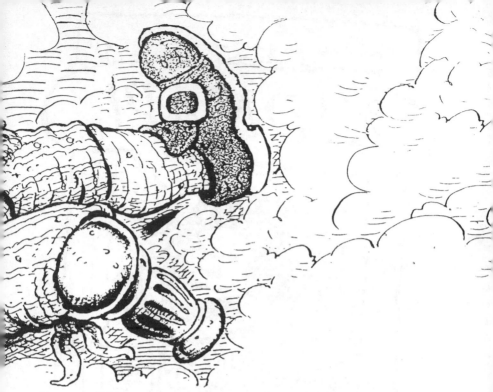

Dear Diary,

Tricked! Betrayed! Duped! Fiddled! Fooled and double-crossed! Last night, after I'd taken Spud for a walk, he ran into the staffroom and I followed him in.

From the shadow of the captain's hammock, hidden by clouds of tobacco smoke, I heard terrible things...

"KIDNAP!" I yelled, when I got back to our quarters. "Captain Abdul and his dirty double-crossing teachers are going to kidnap us tonight and when our mums and dads arrive tomorrow for parents' day, all they will find will be a ransom note! We must do something!"

Arrgh!

"But what?" asked
the kids.

"MUTINY!" said I.
"We get them before
they get us!"

"YES!" everyone
shouted.

"Shush!" I hissed.
"Get your swords and
follow me. Tom, you
bring the ropes."

"Aye-aye, Captain!"
said Tom. "I mean,
yes, Pickles."

Armed to the teeth with swords
and ropes, our fearless band of pirate
pupils crept down to the staffroom.

I gave the order and we attacked!

The battle was over in minutes.
We swarmed all over the pirate
teachers and tied them up with so
much rope they looked like cocoons!

We rolled the teachers out onto the quayside.

One of the kids shouted, "What now?"

"We sail for the West Indies!" I cried. "Who's with me? Who really wants to be a pirate?"

"ME! ME! ME!" they all shouted.

"Good!" said I. "Raid the kitchen, fill the water barrels and get the ship ready. We sail in ten minutes!"

I wrote a note to our parents telling them what had happened, pinned it to Captain Abdul and we set sail.

Dear Diary, (six months later)
This is the life! We now call ourselves "Pirate pirates" because we only steal from other pirates.

On our last raid we found out that pirates from all around the world had heard about our mutiny.

Thinking how well taught we must have been, they have sent their kids to Captain Abdul's school! Abdul claims the mutiny was all his idea – part of his teaching plan. The scoundrel!

And so everybody is happy: Captain
Abdul because his school is a roaring
success and our parents because we
send lots of treasure home.

The kids are happy because they get to sail and swim and fight and fire cannon and rob bullies and stay up all night!

And me? Well,
I paint my pictures
and write my poems
and I'm captain of
my own pirate ship!
Who could ask for
anything more...

I'm Captain
Maisy Pickles –
the happiest girl
in the whole, wide,
wonderful world!

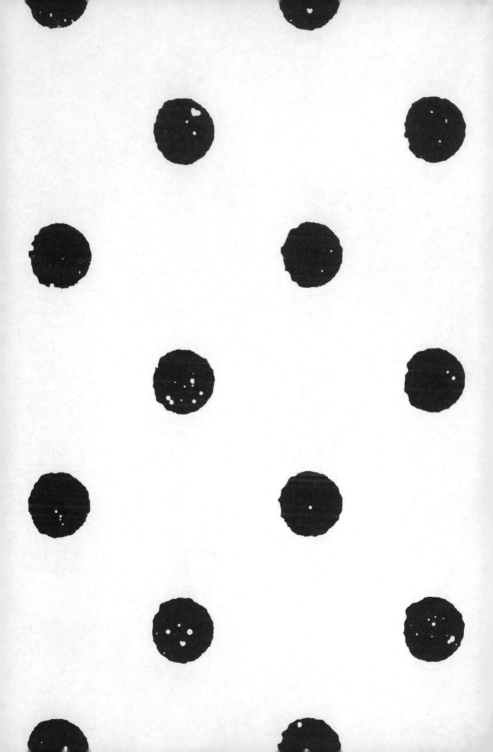